It's Okay to Be Different

TODD PARR

Megan Tingley Books

Little, Brown and Company
Boston New York London

To Megan
for believing in something different
Love,
Todd

ALSO BY TODD PARR:
The Best Friends Book
Big & Little
Black & White
Do's and Don'ts
The Feelings Book
My Really Cool Baby Book
The Okay Book
Things That Make You Feel Good/
Things That Make You Feel Bad
This Is My Hair
Underwear Do's and Don'ts
Zoo Do's and Don'ts

First Edition

Library of Congress Cataloging-in-Publication Data

Parr, Todd.
  It's okay to be different / by Todd Parr. — 1st ed.
  p. cm
  Summary: Illustrations and brief text describe all kinds of differences that are
"okay," such as "It's Okay to be a different color," "It's Okay to need some help,"
"It's Okay to be adopted," and "It's Okay to have a Different nose."
  ISBN 0-316-66603-3
  [1. Self-esteem — Fiction. 2. Individuality — Fiction.] I. Title
PZ7.P2447 It 2001
[E] — dc21   00-042829

10 9 8 7 6 5 4 3 2

TWP

Printed in Singapore

It's okay to be missing a tooth (or two or three)

It's okay to need some help

It's okay to have a

different nose

It's okay to be a different color

It's okay to have no hair

It's okay to have BIG ears

It's okay to have wheels

It's okay to be

Small   Medium

Large   Extra Large

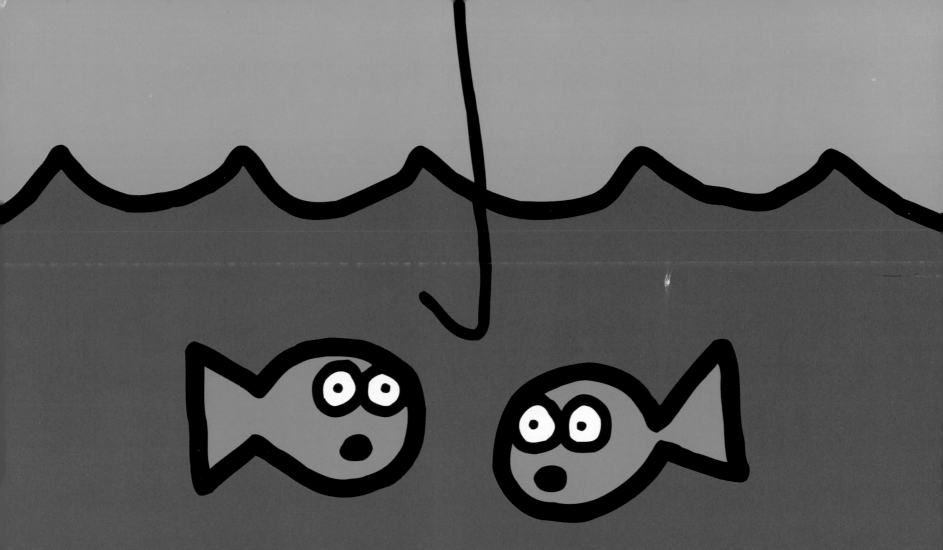

It's okay to say NO
to bad things

It's okay to come
from a different place

It's okay to be embarrassed

It's okay to have a pet worm

It's okay to be proud of yourself

It's okay to have different Moms

It's okay to have different Dads

It's okay to be adopted

It's okay to have an invisible friend

It's okay to do something nice for someone

It's okay to lose
your mittens

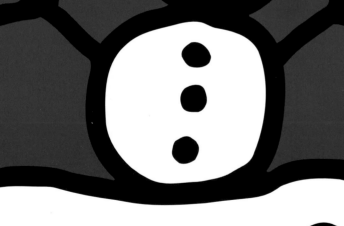

It's okay to help a
squirrel collect nuts

It's okay to have different kinds of friends

It's okay to make a wish

It's Okay to be different. You are Special and Important just because of being who you are.

Love,
Todd